W9-DEM-143

For more than forty years,
Yearling has been the leading name
in classic and award-winning literature
for young readers.

Yearling books feature children's
favorite authors and characters,
providing dynamic stories of adventure,
humor, history, mystery, and fantasy.

Trust Yearling paperbacks to entertain,
inspire, and promote the love of reading
in all children.

OTHER YEARLING BOOKS YOU WILL ENJOY

MATILDA BONE, *Karen Cushman*

BUD, NOT BUDDY, *Christopher Paul Curtis*

PICTURES OF HOLLIS WOODS, *Patricia Reilly Giff*

ALL THE WAY HOME, *Patricia Reilly Giff*

BELLE PRATER'S BOY, *Ruth White*

WHEN ZACHARY BEAVER CAME TO TOWN
Kimberly Willis Holt

ON MY HONOR, *Marion Dane Bauer*

Baby

Patricia MacLachlan

Baby

A Yearling Book

Published by Yearling, an imprint of Random House Children's Books
a division of Random House, Inc., New York

"Dirge Without Music" by Edna St. Vincent Millay. From *Collected Poems*, HarperCollins. Copyright © 1928, 1955 by Edna St. Vincent Millay and Norma Millay Ellis. Reprinted by permission of Elizabeth Barnett, literary executor.

William Carlos Williams: *The Collected Poems of William Carlos Williams, 1909–1939, vol. I.* Copyright © 1938 by New Directions Publishing Corporation. Reprinted by permission of New Directions Publishing Corp.

"Me and My Shadow"—Words and music by Dave Dreyer, Billy Rose, and Al Jolson. Copyright © 1927 by Bourne Co. and Larry Spier, Inc., New York. Reprinted with permission.

Visit us on the Web! www.randomhouse.com/kids

Educators and librarians, for a variety of teaching tools, visit us at www.randomhouse.com/teachers

ISBN: 0-440-41145-9

Reprinted by arrangement with Delacorte Press

Printed in the United States of America

September 1995

40 39 38 37

This book is for Jamie MacLachlan.

I am not resigned to the shutting away of loving hearts
    in the hard ground.
So it is, and so it will be, for so it has been, time out
    of mind:
Into the darkness they go, the wise and the lovely.
    Crowned
With lilies and with laurel they go; but I am not re-
    signed.

—from "Dirge Without Music"
Edna St. Vincent Millay

baby

summer's end

The memory is this: a blue blanket in a basket that pricks her bare legs, and the world turning over as she tumbles out. A flash of trees, sky, clouds, and the hard driveway of dirt and gravel. Then she is lifted up and up and held tight. Kind faces, she remembers, but that might be the later memory of her imagination. Still, when the memory comes, sometimes many times a night and in the day, the arms that hold her are always safe.

chapter 1

In the evenings my father danced. All day long he was quiet and stubborn, the editor of the island newspaper. But in the evenings he danced.

Lalo Baldelli and I sat on the porch swing, clapping our hands over our ears when the six o'clock ferry whistle blew, and inside, as always, my father began to tap-dance on the coffee table. It was a low, tiled table, blue and green Italian marble. My father loved the sound of his taps on the tiles. He danced every evening before dinner, after his six crackers (Ritz) with cheddar cheese (extra sharp), between the first glass of whiskey that made him happy and the second that made

5

him sad. He always began slowly with "Me and My Shadow," then "East Side, West Side," working up to Lalo's favorite, "I Got Rhythm." Wherever he was, Lalo would come to our house before dinner so he wouldn't miss my father's wild and breathless "I Got Rhythm" that finished with a flourish, hands stretched out as if playing to a large audience. Lalo was the only one who applauded, except later, of course, when Sophie did.

There was a rhythm to the rest of my family too. When my father began to dance my mother would come out of her studio, covered with paint if her work was not going well; and Grandma Byrd would come up from her afternoon nap, her hair untouched by sleep.

Today my mother came out onto the porch, carrying a silver bowl that held batter for a cake that would never be baked. She carried spoons for Lalo and me, and the large wooden one for herself.

"You'll like this, Larkin," she said to me, handing me a spoon.

"What kind?" asked Lalo, peering into the bowl.

"Spice," said Mama.

6

"That's much better before it's baked," said Lalo.

Mama smiled at him.

"You bet," she said, taking a huge spoonful, then handing us the bowl.

Mama was covered with flecks and smears of paint, and I could tell by the colors what she was working on. The island. Blue for the water of the island ponds and the sky and the sea; green for the hills—light green for the meadows and fields, dark for the stands of spruce. Mama was a walking landscape. That meant trouble, more paint on Mama than on canvas. That meant she was restless. Mama saw me looking at her clothes.

"I can't concentrate," she said, her voice flat and unhappy.

The porch window behind me opened.

"Are you eating batter?" Byrd asked.

"Spice," said Mama and Lalo at the same time.

The window closed, and we heard Byrd slide open the mahogany pocket doors to her room. She appeared on the porch with her own spoon.

Lalo offered her his seat.

"My dear," she murmured, and sat, holding up her hand in what Mama called her queen's wave.

Byrd grew up in a grand house with pillars and many porches, and could have been a queen. She was seventy years old with white hair piled on her head, and rows of neck wrinkles like necklaces.

Byrd said often that she was pleased to have all her faculties. Once, though, after an island party and some punch, she called them facilities, and some townspeople still believed that she had many bathrooms in the house and that she loved them all. Lately she had discovered fancy stockings. To-day they were black with jewels that sparkled as she moved. The jewels worked like little prisms, tossing light around, causing spots to tremble on the porch ceiling.

"Great socks," said Lalo, making Byrd laugh.

"Stockings, Lalo," she corrected him. "One day you may live off island, you know, and you'll see things you never dreamed of. Including patterned stockings."

Lalo looked at Byrd, horrified, his spoon half-way to his mouth.

8

"Not me," he said. "I'll never leave this island. Everything is here."

Mama smiled wistfully.

"Almost everything," said Byrd. She sighed. "But I do miss—" She stopped suddenly, and I looked at her, waiting for her to say what I knew she missed. What *I* missed.

Mama turned to look at her, too, her eyes sharp and sad at the same time. Then Mama's expression changed as she looked up at Papa, who stood at the doorway, his face all flushed from tap-dancing.

"What?" asked Papa, out of breath. "What do you miss?"

"Something," said Byrd lightly, her tone changing. "I don't know just what, but I miss something."

"I know," said Mama. "I'm restless. Tomorrow the last summer ferry leaves. And then?"

"We get the island back," Papa said, "and everything will be quiet and peaceful and all ours."

"Excitement," said Byrd suddenly, her face bright with memory. "We need something new and exciting to happen."

"Like dinner?" suggested Papa.

"Oh!" Mama jumped up so quickly that the porch swing almost toppled Byrd. "The pot roast is done. Here." She gave the batter bowl to Papa.

"What was this?" he asked, sampling it.

"That was dessert, dear heart," said Byrd. She got up very slowly. Then, with a quick smile and a sudden shake of herself, like a wren, she went inside.

"Such excitement," said Papa softly. Then he looked at us. "This is enough excitement." There was a pause. "Isn't it?" he added, asking himself the question.

We ate dinner as the sun set; candles on the table, the dinner a yearly celebration that tomorrow the island visitors would leave. The seasons on our island rose and fell in a rhythm like the rise and fall of the tides. Autumn was ours with quick colors, leaves flying until they were gone and we could see the shape of the island. The land rose and fell, too, from the north point where the lighthouse stood, curving down into valleys like hands holding pond water.

Soon winter would come, the winds shaking the windows of the house, the sea black. Herring gulls would sit out of the wind on our porch, watching for spring that would come so fast and cold, we would hardly know it was there. Then summer, visitors would come off the ferry again, flooding us, the air heavy with their voices. And again, at summer's end they would be gone like the tide, leaving behind small signs of themselves: a child's pail with a broken handle, a tiny white sock by the water's edge. Bits and pieces of them left like good-byes.

Suddenly, as we ate, a gull flew low over the house, its crazy shriek startling us. We looked up, then at each other. Nervous looks and laughter. But there was nothing to be nervous about on that day.

It was the next day, after the last ferry took the summer people away, that it happened.

chapter 2

Puffs of wind came off the water, sending Lalo's hat flying down the beach. He ran after it, small sprays of sand sent up by his feet. A kite whirled and dipped, suddenly plunging into the water. There was a group sigh behind us, summer tourists on the porch of Lalo's parents' hotel. They stood like birds on a line, their bags all packed, faces red, noses peeling from summer sun. Summer's end.

"Lalo!" Mr. Baldelli called from the porch, and we ran up to carry bags to the hotel truck, hoping for tips.

"My umbrella, don't forget, Larkin," called

Mrs. Bloom. Mrs. Bloom came every summer, bringing her beach umbrella, her chair, and her little hairy dog whose full name was Craig Walter. I took the yellow umbrella from Mrs. Bloom. In her arms Craig bared his teeth at me.

The Willoughbys clutched handfuls of wildflowers, almost gone by. Their children lugged suitcases of rocks, dead horseshoe crabs, and sea urchins that would crumble before they got home.

Lalo and I sat on the back of the truck for the short ride along the beach road to the dock. We passed people on bicycles, their baskets filled. We passed parents walking with children, babies in backpacks, dogs loping nose to the ground behind them.

At the dock cars were already lined up waiting to leave. Griffey and his musical group were there, playing "Roll Out the Barrel," the only song they knew. Griffey played accordion and Rollie the fiddle. Arthur played his saxophone, and old man Brick played only three notes on his bagpipe: major, minor, and "something diminished," as Mama put it.

Papa was there saying good-bye to summer people. I could see the stubble on his face, the

1 3

beginnings of his yearly winter beard that he shaved off every June before the tourists returned. Byrd and Mama were there, too, Byrd's legs sparkling, her hair blown like tossed snow. Mama handed a wrapped package to a woman, then smiled at Lalo and me across the dock because she had sold a painting. A child in overalls ran toward the dock's edge, arms up, until his laughing father caught him up in his arms, swinging him over his head. A young woman holding a baby stood near, watching us. A dogfight began, then ended as owners pulled on their leashes.

The cars, all stuffed with suitcases and sleeping bags and coolers, beach chairs tied on top, began to move onto the ferry. Then the bicycles were wheeled on.

"Good-bye!" called Mrs. Bloom, waving one of Craig's small paws at us.

"Good-bye!" we shouted back.

And the gates were closed with a metal clang, the huge lines tossed on board.

Surprisingly, Griffey, Rollie, Arthur, and old man Brick began a new song.

"Whatever?" exclaimed Mama behind me.

"They've learned something new," cried Lalo.

1 4

"What is it?" I asked.

" 'Amazing Grace,' " said Papa, grinning.

The *Island Queen* moved off, and my mother began to laugh. Byrd sang in her old voice:

Amazing Grace, how sweet the sound,
That saved a wretch like me!
I once was lost, but now am found;
Was blind, but now I see.

As the boat reached the breakwater we all put our hands to our ears as the whistle blew. Above, the sky was ice-blue, low clouds skimming across, and without the noise like one of Mama's paintings. And then it was quiet, a handful of us left: Griffey and the boys packing up their instruments, Lalo's father hosing down his truck at the dock's edge, islanders walking away. A couple I didn't know held hands. Maybe they would fly out tonight on the small plane. The woman holding the baby still watched us. A cloud slipped in front of the sun.

Summer's end.

"Your mom cried," said Lalo as we walked up from the water through the fields.

"She always cries at the end of summer," I said. "At the end of anything. At weddings." I looked at Lalo. "And parades."

Lalo burst out laughing. The Fourth of July parade was led by Griffey's goat and the sewer-pump truck, and still my mama cried.

Lalo and I sat on the rock by the pond. Water bugs skimmed along the surface; a fish jumped, sending out circle after circle. Way off in the distance the ferry was a small dot, getting smaller, a thread of smoke rising from its stack.

"So," said Lalo. Lalo began most sentences with *so*. Ms. Minifred, the school librarian, was trying to break him of the habit.

"Get to it, Lalo," Ms. Minifred said. "You will miss your own marriage when the minister asks you if you take this woman and you begin with *so*. You will miss the end of your life, too, when you try to leave behind some wondrous words."

Ms. Minifred liked wondrous words. She loved the beginnings of books, and the ends. She loved clauses and adverbial phrases and the de-

1 6

scriptions of sunsets and death. Lalo called her "It Was the Worst of Times Minifred."

"You are a full-time job, Lalo," Ms. Minifred told Lalo once after he had asked her twelve questions in a row.

"Thank you, Ms. Minifred," said Lalo, missing the point.

I wondered what she would do when Lalo went off-island to high school. Maybe she would wither away among all the books with all the words in them until no one could ever find her again unless they opened a book. Or, she might ferment in the library like Mama's back-porch cider that finally exploded.

"So," repeated Lalo, "tomorrow you will buy a plaid dress and the year will begin."

I smiled.

My mother believed in plaid. Plaid meant beginnings. Each year I began school with a plaid dress, then slowly that beginning became the past as I wore jeans and shirts, then shorts when it was hot. In my closet hung five plaid dresses, one for each year, like memorials.

"So," I imitated Lalo, getting up from the rock and grabbing a clump of chickory, "tomorrow, yes, I will buy a plaid dress and your mother will buy you a new lunch box."

"And it will be another year like all the other years," said Lalo happily.

His smile made me smile, but I knew he was wrong. All the years were changed because of what I was missing and no one would talk about. And all the years would be changed even more than Lalo and I knew, for when we walked through the meadow of chickory and meadowsweet, when we climbed up and over the rise to my house, the basket was already in the driveway, a baby sitting in it, crying. My mother stood with her hands up to her face, shocked. My father's face was dark and still and bewildered. Only Byrd looked happily satisfied, as if something wonderful, something wished for, had happened.

And it had.

Her excitement was here.

Sometimes she dreamed of white hair, like silk, touching her face, and tiny white stones that tumbled. Beach stones, maybe. And crying. She could almost taste the salt of tears when she thought of it; the taste of memory. Why, then, wasn't she frightened when she remembered this?

chapter 3

The baby looked from one face to the other, then suddenly stopped crying. It was quiet then, no one moving, as if we were actors who had forgotten our lines. Lalo moved in front of me, and I looked over his shoulder at Byrd smiling, my father's dark look, my mother tense and pale. Then, we all turned to watch the baby slowly get up to climb out of the basket. Mama's hands went out protectively, fluttering like birds; Byrd took a step, but the baby, legs twisted in a blanket, fell hard on the driveway and began to wail, a sad sound like a lost cat. In one movement Byrd leaned down and swooped the baby up in her arms, and Mama leaned down and picked up a sheet of paper. The paper fluttered in the breeze. Or was it Mama's hand shaking? Lalo reached back and took my hand, pulling me with him as he moved closer. I knew he was protecting me, but from what? The rest was a scene in slow motion, Papa taking the paper out of my mother's hands, reading it to us, my mother beginning to cry. There was no sound to her crying; only tears streaming down her face. I stared at Mama. *I had never seen Mama cry this way. Terrible, somehow, without the sound.*

My father's voice wavered as he read.

"This is Sophie. She is almost a year old and she is good."

Sophie. At the sound of her name the baby looked up at him and stopped crying. Papa stared at her for a moment. He swallowed, then continued. Lalo pulled me behind him, and as we came closer Sophie turned to look at us. One of her hands went up to rub her ear.

"I cannot take care of her now, but I know she will be safe with you," Papa read. "I have watched you. You will be a good family. I will lose her forever if you don't do this, so please keep her. I will send money for her when I can. I will come back for her one day. I love her."

Lalo still held my hand. Papa looked at Mama.

"She spelled *please* wrong," he said, his voice soft.

Lalo held out his hand to Sophie in Byrd's arms. Sophie stared, then reached out her hand to touch his. Lalo smiled. A small satisfied sound came from Sophie, and she began to move his hand up and down, staring at him as if waiting for something familiar. Lalo took Sophie's other hand and moved it up and down and suddenly, for the first time, Sophie smiled.

Papa turned to Mama, as if Sophie's smile had given him energy.

"Call the police," he said.

Byrd took a breath, almost a gasp.

"We have to report this," said Papa quickly. "This child has been left. This is a criminal act."

Sophie sucked in her breath, imitating Byrd.

Mama didn't answer. She held out her arms to Sophie, and Sophie looked at her steadily, thoughtfully.

"Sophie?" said Mama softly.

She crooned the name, like a lullaby.

Sophie watched Mama. She put two fingers in her mouth; then, after a moment, she took them out.

"Sophie," she repeated, her voice clear and high like a bell.

She lunged toward Mama then, nearly falling out of Byrd's arms. Mama's arms went around her.

"Lily." Papa's voice was loud. "We need to talk inside. Alone, without the baby."

"Without *Sophie*, John," Mama corrected him.

"Without Sophie," said Papa slowly.

"Sophie," repeated Sophie in her small voice.

Mama smiled and so did Byrd, and they looked at each other as if there were a secret between them, something we didn't know.

"Here," said Mama, handing over Sophie to Byrd. "I'm going inside to speak about criminal acts."

"Oh, boy," whispered Lalo beside me. "Oh, boy."

It was quiet outside, warm and peaceful. No clouds cluttered up the sky. Lalo and I sat in the grass with Sophie, playing patty-cake.

"She knows how," said Lalo with an amazed smile.

"All babies know how," said Byrd. She looked at me. "Someone who loves them always teaches them."

She sat on the steps in her dress and fancy stockings watching Sophie and trying to pretend that there were no sounds of loud voices coming from inside. We could hear Papa's voice, strong and sometimes fierce, then Mama's, that sweet soft way of talking she had when she was serious and angry, like a steady hum.

All of a sudden the voices stopped and the silence made us look up. The door opened. Mama came out first, then Papa. Papa looked tired, the way he looked when he had finished his nightly tap dancing.

Byrd stood up and stared at Mama. Sophie turned and put out one arm toward Mama.

"She will stay with us for a while," said Mama softly.

"Until we can come to some civilized agreement about what to do," said Papa firmly.

Byrd smiled. Papa sat down on the porch steps wearily.

"Oh, boy," said Lalo for the third time.

Byrd lifted Sophie and whirled her around until Sophie laughed. A small island plane flew over our heads and away. And Byrd's pearls broke, showering Sophie and falling over the meadow grasses like tears.

chapter 4

It was night, Sophie's first night with us. Moonlight was sliding slowly across my quilt like the tide when I heard her first whimper. There was the scurry of feet, a door opening, then closing, my mother's soft, soothing voice. I turned over and lay looking out the window. Stars were tossed across the sky, a moon nearly full with a small slice off one side. Sophie cried harder, and then a door opened and closed again. I raised my head off the pillow and listened. A new sound came up the stairs. The crying stopped, but I knew the new sound well. I got up and went to the door, opening it. A night-light lighted the hallway. I walked down the cool wood floor, down the stairs, and stopped, my hand on the newel post. One lamp glowed in the living room. Mama sat on the floor holding Sophie. Sophie's face was tear streaked, a sleep line across one cheek. But she stared at my father, her mouth open. His hair was rumpled and his eyes dark circled. He was dressed in pajamas and tap shoes, and he danced on the tiled table. Mama sang along with him.

Boys and girls together.
Me and Mamie O'Rorke
Tripped the light fantastic
On the sidewalks of New York.

Papa ended and Mama clapped for him. Sophie still stared at him, her mouth open. Papa got down off the table and Sophie began to clap too.

"Mo," she said. "Mo."

"More," explained Mama.

Papa sighed.

"I know what *mo* means, Lily," he said grumpily.

He looked over and saw me sitting on the lowest step of the stairway.

"I know what *mo* means," he repeated.

He smiled at me suddenly and I smiled back. We were thinking of all the times that Papa danced for me; all the nighttime songs when I was sick, and how hard he had tried to teach me the soft shoe that I couldn't learn.

Sophie yawned, and Mama stood up with her. Sophie laid her head on Mama's shoulder.

"Thank you," Mama whispered to Papa.

She walked past me on the stairway. Sophie's eyes were already closed.

Papa sighed and walked to the screen door, opening it, walking out onto the porch. I followed him.

He sat on the porch steps. I sat next to him.

"Stars," he said to me.

I nodded. I knew that talk of the stars was in place of things we would not say.

"Milky Way," I said. I pointed. "The Pleiades."

Papa put his arm around me.

"Has anyone asked you what *you* think about all of this?"

"Mama doesn't ask those things," I said to

him sharply. "Not anymore." The sound of anger in my voice surprised me.

"No," his voice was soft. "But I am asking."

"I never had—" I stopped. "I never had a sister," I said slowly. I looked up at Papa and knew that we were both thinking about something else. *Someone* else.

"That's not the question, Lark," said Papa softly.

Insects buzzed in the grass. A gull cried far away over the water.

"I like Sophie," I said. "I don't love her."

"Don't," said Papa. "Don't love her."

He sighed.

"I like her too," he said after a moment.

"Mama will love her soon," I whispered.

"If not already," murmured Papa.

"I'm scared," I said after a while. "For Mama."

There was a silence.

"Yes," said Papa. "But it is not your job to protect her."

I looked up at Papa.

"Is it your job?" I asked.

Papa didn't speak for a moment.

29

"Not if she won't let me," he said.

We sat for a long time then, watching clouds fall over the moon like nets. After a while I knew there weren't any more words. Not now. I got up and went inside, up the stairs to bed. Soon, just before I fell asleep, I heard the sound downstairs of ice in a glass and then, like messages, my father's dancing. I listened half the night to his taps on the tiles as the moon moved across the sky and away.

"So?" said Lalo at the door. He grinned his crazy morning grin. He probably slept smiling.

My eyes squinted against the hard morning light.

"In the kitchen," I said.

Lalo walked past me. I stood, looking out into the sunlight. Then I slammed the door.

"Good morning to you too," I said, my voice so loud that I surprised myself.

"Hi, Larkin," he called to me over his shoulder before he disappeared into the kitchen.

"So, Sophie!" I heard him say. "It's Lalo!"

I heard Sophie's delighted "La."

I walked into the kitchen and leaned against the counter. Morning sun came in, pouring over Mama's glass bottles in the window. Byrd sat in her velvet bathrobe, the wrinkles on her face like etched glass in the sunlight. Papa drank orange juice as he read the newspaper. Sophie sat in my old high chair, cereal on her face. She grinned at me suddenly.

"La!" she called, holding out her spoon for me.

I couldn't help smiling back at her. Her tiny neat rows of teeth looked like seed pearls in one of Byrd's brooches. And it came to me, then, like the sudden sharp pain in my chest when I swam too fast, that I was not only scared for Mama, I was scared for me. I looked at Papa and he stared back at me. His look was almost like a warning that said, *Don't, Lark. Don't.*

Lalo saw Papa's expression and his smile faded.

I turned and went out of the kitchen and out onto the porch where there was space. I walked down the steps and out onto the lawn, but I could still hear Sophie's high, happy voice. After a moment I went down past the pond and through the

3 1

fields to the small cemetery that sat on a hill by the water where all I could hear was the sound of the sea and the wind. A tiny stone sat there, surrounded by big headstones with angels and flowers and names engraved on them. There was no name on the tiny stone, just the word BABY and a date that showed that the one buried there had only lived for one day. I felt a movement beside me, and Lalo was there.

"So, Larkin," Lalo began, his voice thin, the words almost blowing away in the wind.

I shook my head. I wanted to talk, but Lalo and I had talked about this many times. It was Mama and Papa I wanted to talk with, but Mama and Papa didn't talk. Not about this.

Beside me Lalo sighed. The wind rippled the unmown grasses. And we stood, silently looking down at the stone that marked the grave of my baby brother.

Most of all she remembered the man. His hands, strong, brown. She could feel the rumble in his chest when he held her, the sound of song coming up through him and surrounding her, making her smile. Even now she smiled at the thought of it. Sometimes in a crowd of people she would hear a voice, turn, look for him. It was not so much his face she looked for.

It was his hands she remembered.

chapter 5

Rock, paper, scissors. Papa tried to teach Sophie the game. They sat on the porch, Sophie in his lap, as Papa held out his hands time after time.

"Rock, paper, see paper, Sophie? Scissors?"

Papa knew she was too young. She couldn't know that paper covered rock, rock crushed scissors, scissors cut paper, but Papa didn't care. Neither did Sophie. There was something about Papa's hands she liked, watching them form rock, paper, scissors. He hid his hands behind his back, and it was not what shape the hands took when they came out of hiding, it was his hands, no matter what, that Sophie liked.

"Mo," said Sophie.

My mother smiled from the porch swing.

"We should teach her words," she said. "Hands, Sophie. Hands."

"Mo," said Sophie, frowning at her.

Papa laughed at the frown and Sophie laughed, too, the sound like water falling over rocks.

"Papa," said my mother. "Say, 'Papa.'"

Slowly, very slowly, Papa stood up. He set Sophie on the porch. He turned to my mother and his quiet anger caused Sophie to stare up at him.

"I'm sorry," said my mother quickly. "I didn't mean that, John."

"Yes, you did, Lily," said Papa. "You meant it. I am not her papa. I am *not*. Somewhere"—his voice faltered and he tried to steady it—"somewhere there is a man who *is* her father. And sometime, maybe soon, her mother will come back for her. She is not yours, Lily. She is *not ours*." He paused and when he spoke again his voice sounded rough, like rock scraping rock. "Sophie is not a substitute," he said slowly.

Mama's mouth opened, then shut. My skin

felt like ice suddenly, the way it felt the day of the first spring swim in the bay.

"I'm sorry, Lily," Papa said softly. "It had to be said."

Papa turned and walked down the steps and down the grass to the path that went to town. Sophie held out a hand to him, but his back was turned and he didn't see. My mother stood up and went after him.

Byrd sighed.

"Ah, well. Here we are, alone at last, Sophie," said Byrd, trying to be cheerful.

Byrd turned to Lalo, then to me, her eyes bright with sudden tears.

"This is not meant to be easy," she said. "It is a very important thing to do, for Sophie and especially for your mother and father. But it will not be easy. Do you understand?"

I understood. I did. I knew that what she meant was what Papa had said. Sophie was not ours. Someday she would go away. Another thing to miss.

"Why is it important?" I asked her.

I asked her for me, but mostly for Lalo, who

36

was holding Sophie as if he would never let her go.

"It is important, Larkin, because we are giving Sophie something to take away with her when she goes."

"What?" asked Lalo. "What will she take with her?"

Sophie looked at Lalo and put her fingers up to his lips to feel them move.

"Us," said Byrd firmly.

"And what will we have when she's gone?" I asked.

Byrd looked at me and shook her head because she couldn't speak.

The sun came out suddenly from behind a cloud. Sophie held up her arms to it. And then Lalo asked what none of us had dared to say out loud.

"What if," Lalo said, looking at Sophie, "what if her mother never comes back?"

Byrd studied Lalo for a moment, then looked out to sea as if there was something important out there. She whispered her answer.

"What?" asked Lalo, leaning toward her.

"She will, Lalo," said Byrd. "She *will* come back."

It was late when Mama and Papa came home. Lalo and I had spent the afternoon trying to teach Sophie words. *Good-bye. Larkin. Lalo. Hands.* Byrd and Lalo were setting the table for supper. I sat on the porch, Sophie sleeping in my arms, when I saw them come up the path from town. They walked slowly up the grass, my father ahead of my mother. Sophie sighed in my lap. I put my arms around her tighter, watching. My mother's face was set, my father's sad.

Sophie woke without crying and sat up, looking at me. Then she turned and saw them. She reached out to my father.

She spoke, the word as clear as an autumn sky.

"Hands," she said.

chapter 6

We could not keep Sophie a secret, a small child at our house. We tried inventing stories.

"A niece?" suggested Papa. "A long-lost niece."

"A cousin," said Mama. "A cousin's baby, left for the winter."

"That sounds like hibernation," said Papa.

"Maybe a crown princess," said Byrd with sarcasm, "dropped from a balloon."

So we stopped trying and told the truth. And Sophie became the island's child, loved by everyone, fed by everyone, baby-sat by everyone, read to and carried about and sung to by all.

We took her to Dr. Unfortunato, as Byrd called him, because of his wife who talked too much. His name was really Dr. Fortunato, and Sophie blew into his stethoscope and made him smile. He read the note from Sophie's mother.

He handed Mama back the note. He looked closely at her.

"How are you with this?" he asked softly.

"Fine," said Mama. "Fine," she said louder.

Dr. Fortunato glanced at Papa quickly, then at Sophie.

"Sophie is healthy," he said. "Has she walked yet?"

"Not by herself," said Mama.

"She climbs the furniture," I said.

"She dances on my feet, holding on," said Papa.

Dr. Fortunato smiled.

"Call me when she does the soft shoe," he said.

Sophie liked carrots and didn't like milk. Beets were for spitting. She hated baths, screaming so hard we had to shut the windows so no one would hear, but she loved to sit in the bay until her skin wrinkled, pouring water from one bucket to another. She napped with Byrd in the afternoons, and Byrd sang every song she knew to Sophie: lullabies, show tunes, hymns, folk songs, and once, in a loud and happy voice, something about a drunken sailor until Papa knocked on the window for her to stop.

School began, and I went off the first day. No plaid dress.

"How come?" I asked Mama.

Mama saw my expression.

"But, Lark, I thought you always hated those plaid dresses," she said.

"I did," I said. "I do."

I smiled at Mama, but my thoughts startled me.

But I wanted one anyway, Mama.

Sophie cried when I left. She sat in her pajamas, her arms stretched up to me, her lower lip jutted out.

"La!" she cried mournfully.

"La!" Sophie said, smiling, when Lalo came to walk to school with me.

"I could stay home from school," I said.

"You'll do no such thing," said Mama. "She'll learn that you come back."

At school the library had been freshly painted, the smell of paint mixing with the smell of old books. The shelves were dusted, the books neatly lined up as if daring us to take them down and read them. Ms. Minifred was slicked and clean and ready for us.

"Good morning. Sit up straight, Lalo," she said. "Slumping may stop the blood from going to your brain."

Lalo grinned. Under the library table was his new lunch box, black and shiny like Ms. Minifred's hair. For Lalo another year like all the other years.

"This year we will be talking about the power of language," said Ms. Minifred. "The power of words. And how words can change you."

I stared at Ms. Minifred.

What about when there are no words? I thought. *Silence can change you, too, Ms. Minifred.*

Ms. Minifred looked at me, as if she had read my thoughts.

"Words," she said.

She looked away, out the library windows, as if she was hearing words from far away. Then she waved her arm at the library shelves.

"In this room, in these books, there is the power of a hundred hurricanes. Wondrous words," said Ms. Minifred.

Lalo and I looked at each other and smiled. Another year.

Mama was right. Sophie was waiting for us at home, her face pressed against the window, when Lalo and I came up the porch steps at the end of the school day.

The second week of school Sophie took her first step, pushing off from Papa's tiled tap-dancing table. Papa clapped, Byrd smiled, Mama cried, and from then on Sophie walked; sometimes tilted forward as if a wind pushed her; sometimes tottering so that our hands went out to protect her.

Sophie rode the island's dirt roads on a seat on the back of Mama's bicycle, pointing to dogs and cats. She learned to wave by cupping her hand and waving to herself. She learned what the word

43

hot meant when she touched the oven door, and that *no* meant *no* when she went near Mama's wet canvases.

And then very suddenly one day she began to put her hands behind her back and bring them out in fists, hands flat, or two-fingered shapes.

"Rock, paper, scissors," said Papa softly. "Sophie learned. She doesn't know what it means, but she learned."

Mama smiled.

"That's how it is with children," said Byrd. She paused. "Someday, she will remember all of this in some way, you know."

We looked at Byrd, then at Sophie. Mama turned from the window, her smile fading, all of us thinking of Sophie's mother. Papa watched Mama. It was as if Byrd, in one sentence, had pulled Sophie back from us to a place where we couldn't follow.

Sophie got up unsteadily and looked at Papa. She picked up one foot and put it down. She did it again.

"The shuffle," whispered Mama. "She wants you to dance."

Mama watched Papa.

"She wants you to dance," she repeated, her voice so thin, it almost broke.

There was a silence. Then Papa leaned over and picked up Sophie. Slowly he began to dance holding her, Sophie beginning to grin at him. But Papa didn't grin back at her. He looked at Mama as he sang.

Me and my shadow
Strolling down the avenue.
Me and my shadow,
Not a soul to tell our troubles to.
And when it's twelve o'clock,
We climb the stair;
We never knock
For nobody's there.

Papa and Sophie danced a long time, the late afternoon light falling over them like a spotlight. Mama watched, standing by the window. Byrd sat, straight as a tree. Only Lalo smiled.

"Come, Larkin," called Papa. "Dance with us."

I shook my head. "I can't," I said.

The next day Sophie's letter came, almost as if

Byrd's words about Sophie's mother had made it happen. Five one-dollar bills slipped out of the letter in Mama's hand as she read.

> *Dear Sophie,*
>   *Happy birthday. I love you. I think of you every hour, every minute of every day.*
>   *Don't forget me.*
>   *Love,*
>   *Mama.*

winter

She loved the wind and she loved music. She remembered them together; the sound of the wind in the marsh grass and a song that she dreamed, a thread sound of song that she couldn't remember when she woke.

chapter 7

Winter came fast with a surprising sudden snow the day before Thanksgiving. We bought Sophie a snowsuit, red boots, and mittens, knowing that the snow would never last. Island snow never lasted. Sophie didn't like the mittens; she didn't like the snowsuit; she didn't like snow. Sophie did like her red rubber boots, shuffling around the house in them during the day, taking them to bed with her that night.

We ate Thanksgiving dinner in the dining room; the glasses gleaming, candles lighted, Sophie in her red boots. Dr. Fortunato stopped by on his way to see Rollie's wife, who had a temperature,

49

but he really came to see Sophie. Griffey came to eat with us, and he played his accordion for Sophie. She liked "Roll Out the Barrel" and loved "Amazing Grace."

"Mo," said Sophie. "Mo."

"You'd better learn some new songs," said Byrd.

"I'm working on it," said Griffey, insulted. "The sewer business is busy, you know."

Griffey began to play "Amazing Grace" again.

"She loves this song," he said to Byrd. "She does."

Byrd nodded.

"She has taste, this child," said Byrd.

Later we walked to town, everyone coming out to say hello and to wave to Sophie and to call happy Thanksgiving from their porches. The light sat like porcelain on the water; the sea calm, the sky the gray of silver-dollar plants.

That night Papa danced good-night for Sophie, dancing "Me and My Shadow" over and over. Lalo taught Sophie how to blow a kiss. Mama got out her sketchbook and began to draw Sophie, the lamp spilling light over her work. I looked over her shoulder as she drew Sophie, all rounded edges, and then the sharper larger figure of Papa holding her.

"Do you think she remembers?" I asked her suddenly.

Mama looked up at me. Her eyes shone bright.

"Remembers?"

"Remembers her mother," I said. "Do you think she misses her?"

Mama stared at me.

"I don't know," she said after a moment. "But it doesn't matter, Larkin. We're doing the right thing." Mama sat back and looked at me. "You know that, don't you? Sometimes you have to do what is right."

What is right. I didn't answer, but I felt my face grow hot with sudden anger. There were words in the spaces between us; those words we had never spoken, words about what *I* thought was right. It was hard to say what I thought without getting rid of those words first. Mama, staring at me as if she knew my thoughts, suddenly straightened her shoulders and went back to her drawing. Conversation was over, that one subject that stood be-

5 1

tween us closed. I watched her sketch, hating the look of her hand slipping across the paper as if she was brushing away all the words I needed to hear. Papa and Sophie came to life on the page, the two of them sitting in a chair by the fireplace now; Sophie imitating Papa—*rock, paper, scissors*—her hands, almost like Mama's: quick shadows like butterflies in the firelight.

"They never named him," I said.

We stood on Lalo's favorite place on the island, the north cliffs that stood high above the water. Lalo liked the high places, the dangerous edges of the island that always scared me. *He isn't afraid of anything.* Lalo looked at me for a moment. His hair blew across his face. He turned, then threw a rock out over the water. He leaned down to watch the rock disappear, a tiny splash from where we stood. I shivered and pulled my hat down over my ears, hooking my fingers in Lalo's belt as I always did.

Lalo straightened and smiled at me. This was his favorite cold, windy weather, too, and he only wore a sweatshirt.

52

"I won't fall, Larkin. I never fall, so stop worrying. Remember? Once I slept in a tree."

I remembered. His mother had once taken him to a new barber who cut Lalo's hair too short. Lalo hid from everyone, spending a day and a night up the tree by the pond until his mother lured him down with kale soup and cake.

"You haven't fallen yet," I said. I looked out at the water, gray and dark, whitecaps everywhere. "But things happen when you don't think they will. Things happen that you've never even thought about. Ever."

We began to walk the cliff path toward town.

"So," said Lalo. I could see his breath hang in a cloud. "It's only been six months since he"— Lalo looked sideways at me before he finished— "since he died. Mama said it takes people time. She says it's different for different people."

I didn't say anything. Lalo picked up another rock and drew back his arm to throw it.

"Why didn't they name him?" I asked.

Lalo paused, then threw the rock way out over the water.

"So," he said, his hair lifting strangely in the wind, "*you* name him."

I stopped.

"What?"

"You always do that," said Lalo. "You always say, 'What?' when you don't know what to say. Or you don't want to answer. The fact is, if you need him named, then you name him."

I stared at Lalo and he stared back. Then he turned and began walking again. I stood, watching him as he walked down through the beach plum; past the clumps of chickory gone by; past the juniper bushes.

"You're dumb," I yelled at Lalo. "You're so dumb. The very dumbest!"

The sky darkened above suddenly, a cloud in front of the sun, like in a movie when it was suddenly serious and you'd better pay attention. Lalo disappeared over the hill and I stopped yelling. Then, after a moment, he appeared, looking at me.

I looked at the sea again, then I walked after him. When I reached him he was sitting by the old scrub oak tree that perched at the edge of the cliff.

I stood next to him and looked down on the town. I could see a car moving along Main Street, the church spire in the middle, a fishing boat coming into the harbor.

"It wouldn't matter, you know," I said. "It wouldn't matter as much, except—" I stopped.

Lalo looked up at me.

"Except that Sophie's here," he said.

Tears came then, I couldn't stop them, flooding down my face, cold and startling. Lalo didn't move. He didn't come over to put his arm around me, or put his hand on my arm. He just stared out over the water. And I cried, thinking about what my father had said to me not so long ago.

"Don't love her," he had said to me about Sophie.

Don't worry, Papa. I don't know how to love Sophie. I don't know how to love Sophie because I don't know how to love my brother.

I cried.

Lalo sat under the tree, not looking at me.

The sun came out.

chapter 8

"My Wish for the World."

Portia Pinter stood in front of the class, reading in her high voice.

Someone snorted.

Ms. Minifred gave a piercing look to the back, probably to Ozzie, who always snorted. He had four brothers who snorted too. Lalo said it was part of the family tradition.

"My Wish for the World," repeated Portia, pushing up her glasses, "is for world peace and homes for stray animals, especially cats."

Another snort. Ms. Minifred smiled.

Portia, short with jeweled eyeglasses, had told

us once she had relatives in the royal family of England. Lalo called her Princess Portia.

Portia's voice droned on. We were in the library, where water was leaking down the walls. It had rained for three days straight, so hard and fierce that at home Mama put towels on the windowsills and under the door where the water streamed in. Papa left early for work and came home in the evening wearing his yellow slicker, the wind nearly blowing him down the hill. Byrd sang songs and read books to Sophie, who happily pointed out new streams of water.

At school we had all helped move the books to the middle of the room, and Rebel, the janitor, had come up from the basement to turn off the electricity. Rebel had come to the island with his Harley-Davidson motorcycle when he was eighteen and had never left. That was fifteen years ago. We had seen pictures of him then, and he hadn't changed. He was still thin, and his hair stood straight up. He had a mysterious tattoo on his arm that said "Wild Eunice."

Rebel liked Ms. Minifred. Rebel and Ms. Minifred read books together. Lalo and I had come late to the school library one afternoon, and they had been at a library table, Rebel sitting on a child's chair, smiling, his chin resting on his knees as he read to Ms. Minifred.

Rebel had a bookcase in the basement filled with books. Lalo had seen it once when he went down to borrow a screwdriver.

"All poetry," Lalo had said, impressed.

"That's because Rebel is anguished," said Portia. "All anguished people read poetry. He has a lost love somewhere. Eunice, you know. Ms. Minifred is helping him through the power of wondrous words."

Ozzie snorted.

"He has lots of loves," he scoffed. "I've seen him around town with girls on the back of his Harley."

"They are only temporary," said Portia, her jeweled glasses gleaming in the darkened room, "until Wild Eunice returns."

Today Rebel stood at the back, listening to Portia, his tool chest at his feet, his arms folded so we could see Wild Eunice on his arm; red letters with green ivy surrounding them in a violent sort of way. He had never stayed in class before. He

58

had always come to work, then disappeared back into his room in the basement. I thought suddenly of the day that Griffey's goat had jumped his fence and walked through town and into the school, a strange sight in the schoolroom, interrupting the familiar rhythm of the class. Somehow Rebel seemed too big for the room, filling it up with leather and spiked hair.

Rebel saw me watching him, and he mouthed the words *How's Sophie?*

Fine, I mouthed back. *Walking.*

Rebel smiled broadly.

"Also," Portia went on, "it would be quite excellent to have clean air, clean water, and clean houses. In conclusion," said Portia, stopping to take a breath, "cleanliness is next to godliness."

Portia looked at the class. "My mother says so," she added.

A snort from the back.

"Thank you, Portia," said Ms. Minifred.

"There's redundancy there," said Rebel.

Everyone turned to look at Rebel, who never spoke up when he was in the room.

"Yes, most assuredly there is," said Ms.

59

Minifred. "You don't need to say 'quite excellent,' Portia. *Excellent* is its own definition. It stands alone."

"Yep," said Rebel, picking up his toolbox and pausing at the door to look at Ms. Minifred. "It doesn't get any better than excellent."

There was what Ms. Minifred called a "pulsing silence" as Rebel went out the door. Then Ms. Minifred spoke.

"Yep, indeed," said Ms. Minifred, her face flushed. "Wondrous words spoken by Rebel. It doesn't get any better than excellent."

Lalo and I looked at each other. It was, of course, the *yep* that did it. In that moment, the room so damp that my hair had begun to curl on its own, Lalo and I knew that there was more than words between Rebel and Ms. Minifred.

Lalo leaned over to whisper.

"So. Do you think anyone else noticed?"

I shook my head. Everyone else was rustling papers.

"Poor Ms. Minifred if Wild Eunice ever finds out," I whispered back.

Lalo grinned suddenly at me, then at Ms. Minifred.

"I think Ms. Minifred can take care of herself," he said softly.

And then, Ms. Minifred looked up suddenly and smiled at us. A real smile, with teeth.

"Tomorrow is poetry," she said. Her smile grew wider. "All the world can be found in poetry. All you need to see and hear. All the moments, good and bad, joyous and sad."

Lalo leaned close to me.

"Rebel will be back," he whispered.

All the world.

Lalo and I walked home through town, the wind pushing us along, our feet wet even though we wore rubber boots. The harbor was black, waves topped with gray. We passed the newspaper building, and I looked in and saw Papa reading at his desk, his reading lamp shining on the wood. We passed the hardware store and the drugstore and FOOD MART with the D missing so it read FOO MART.

I pulled my slicker around me and held my rain hat on to keep it from blowing away.

All you need to see and hear.

6 1

Lalo tugged at my arm.

"What?"

"Home," said Lalo.

I looked up and saw the inn, the porch all wet and windswept. Lalo pulled me up the steps, and we took off our hats, standing there, listening to the rain on the porch roof.

"So?" Lalo said.

"I'm thinking about poetry," I said.

"I knew that," said Lalo matter-of-factly.

"And what Ms. Minifred said."

Lalo nodded.

"And I'm thinking about—" I began.

"The world," said Lalo.

I looked at Lalo.

"Poetry is just words," I said.

"That's all we've got," said Lalo.

I stared at Lalo. The rain came harder.

And when I left Lalo and ran up through the wind and rain to my house and opened the door, Mama and Sophie were at the kitchen table, Sophie covered with finger paint, her fingers squishing the red on the white paper. My mother turned, and on her face were tiny finger marks where Sophie had touched her. They had dried there as if

62

she had left her marks on Mama forever. They both smiled at me, and Sophie reached out her hands to touch me too.

Ms. Minifred's wrong, I thought, as I left my slicker dripping in the hallway and went to join them. *There are no words for this.*

She remembered the color red: red flowers that bloomed in winter, cold red sunsets, and especially a tiny teardrop of red that glowed like fire in the light. She now wore it around her neck, but when she thought of it she could remember the feel of it in her hand, how her fingers curled around it. Sometimes she opened her hand, expecting to see it there shining in the pocket of her palm.

Red had always made her happy.

chapter 9

In the night I woke to hear the rain turn to ice, the sound like rocks against the roof and windows. When I slept again I dreamed. I was cold in my dream, so cold that goose bumps rose on my arms, and when I breathed out my breath hung in a cloud of ice. In my dream the fields were ice covered, the sea was frozen, the waves spiking in gleaming glass waves. Far off Sophie was walking away from the island in her red boots.

"Baby!" I called to her, but she didn't turn around. She walked across the harbor, around the fishing boats frozen in place.

"Come back, Baby!" I screamed.

In my dream Byrd came to stand next to me.

"Call her by her name," Byrd said sadly. "Call her Sophie."

Tears sat frozen on her cheeks like diamonds. I stared at her, but when I turned back it was too late. Sophie had walked past the breakwater and was gone.

"La."

Fingers poked at my eyes.

"La."

I woke in the darkened room, the dream slipping away. Sophie sat on my bed in her blue woolly pajamas with the feet. Her red boots were next to my pillow.

"La."

Sophie's cold fingers touched the tears on my cheeks.

I sat up in bed. The air was cold in my bedroom, though early light shone in along the edges of the window shades. I leaned over and pulled up the shade. Ice sat thick on the inside of the windows. Outside there was ice everywhere, the telephone lines and the roads covered, the trees bending over with the weight. The fields were still and shining, like my dream.

I pulled Sophie under the covers with me, tucking them around us.

"Sophie!" Mama called down the hallway.

"Sophie!" called Sophie, imitating her.

"There you are," said Mama in the doorway. "The electricity is off, Larkin. Papa's making a fire. You'd better stay in bed until we get some heat in the living room."

Mama came over close to the bed and looked down at us. Behind her Byrd appeared, dressed in her velvet robe, heavy socks, earrings, and a hat. I smiled.

"Don't mention how I look," warned Byrd.

"Brrr," said Sophie, reaching out a hand to her.

"She said Byrd!" said Mama, smiling at Byrd. "Sophie's beginning to say more than her name. At last!"

"Lily! The fire's ready." Papa's voice came from downstairs.

Mama turned and went down the hallway, pulling her sweater around her.

Byrd sat on my bed and took Sophie's hand.

"Hand," said Sophie.

"No school," Byrd said to me.

I sighed.

"No poetry," I said.

After a moment I looked at Byrd.

"What do you know about poetry?" I asked Byrd.

Byrd smiled and shivered. I opened the covers for her and she got in, Sophie between us. Sophie reached over and played with the ruby that hung on the gold chain around Byrd's neck.

"Poetry is a way of taking life by the throat," said Byrd. "That's what Robert Frost said."

"Ms. Minifred says that poetry shows us the world," I said.

Byrd smiled.

"Words are uppermost in Ms. Minifred's life," she said.

"Do you think words have answers?" I asked.

Byrd took off her necklace and handed it to Sophie.

"La," said Sophie happily.

She looked at it closely, turning it over and over in her hand.

"Do you?" I asked Byrd. "Think words have answers?"

"It depends on your questions," said Byrd. "But"—she turned her head to look at me over Sophie—"you should know that there are some things for which there are no answers, no matter how beautiful the words may be."

I stared at her.

"Sometimes poetry—words—give us a small, lovely look at ourselves," said Byrd. "And sometimes that is enough."

There was silence.

"Sometimes," Byrd added in a soft voice.

"I had a dream," I said. "You were in it."

"A good dream?"

"No," I said. "Sophie walked away across the icy sea and never once looked back at us."

Byrd was quiet, and we watched Sophie open and close her small hand around the ruby. After a moment Byrd sighed.

"That's the way it will be, Larkin," she said.

"In the dream I called Sophie Baby. You told me to call her by her name," I said.

"Baby," said Sophie, putting her hand on my lips.

"Baby," I said, smiling at her.

We lay in silence, the three of us, as the sun rose and came in through the window and over us. Outside the island glistened.

"Why didn't Mama and Papa name the baby?" I asked.

Byrd didn't look surprised.

"Have you asked them?"

I shook my head.

"No," said Byrd. "For now it is too new, too close to them to talk about. They are busy trying to protect each other."

She turned and looked at me.

"You are wondering right now who is protecting *you*, aren't you?" she asked.

I didn't answer. Sophie came out from under the covers.

"I never saw the baby, Byrd," I whispered. "Not once. And he doesn't have a name."

"I know." Byrd whispered too. "But that is for your mama and papa to do. You will have to find your way. Your dream is like a poem, you know. It put in words what you think about but can't say. Maybe that's what poems do. Maybe this is what Ms. Minifred knows."

I looked out the window for a moment, then I turned back to Byrd.

"Byrd?"

"Yes, dear."

"Words are not uppermost in Ms. Minifred's life anymore."

"Is that so?"

"Ms. Minifred and Rebel are in love. She said 'yep' yesterday. Just like Rebel."

At this Byrd raised her head off the pillow.

"She said 'yep'?"

"Yep," I said.

Byrd began to laugh, and I laughed too. Sophie peered at us, sitting back on her heels, smiling.

"Baby," I said. "Hello, Baby."

The smells of coffee and toast cooking in the fireplace came up from downstairs. And Byrd and I lay in bed with the sun coming in across the quilt, watching Sophie open and close her hand over the ruby.

Open, close. Open, close. Open, close.

chapter 10

Six days of ice.

Six days of no electricity.

No school because of water leaks.

And then, suddenly, without any warning, Sophie began to speak in sentences.

We'd spent hours in front of the fireplace. We'd eaten toast cooked over the fire and soup from the soup pot, when Sophie stood up and looked at us and said, "Food not good."

Lalo loved it. He had come over to our house, wrapped like a mummy. He wore a wool hat, wool gloves, wool-lined boots, and a great wool scarf that Byrd said could have covered his mother's grand piano. Mama laughed when she opened the door.

"Lalo? Are you in disguise?"

"My mother," explained Lalo as he came in quickly. "She thinks germs cannot penetrate wool. Her words."

Papa and Mama smiled. Lalo's mother, Marvella, was efficient, running a forty-two-room inn. She was also beautiful and tall with long black hair, and she had come to the island fifteen years ago and fallen in love right off with Lalo's father, who was then a fisherman. She had convinced him to buy the inn.

"I don't want you to fish. I'm scared of water. It makes me sick," she had said.

"But this is an island, surrounded by water," he'd told her.

I thought Marvella was perfect, and brave to be living in a place that scared her because she loved Lalo's father. Even her name was perfect, Marvella Baldelli. She cooked dishes with wonderful names, too, like *Provençale* and *scallopini* and *francese*. She did, however, have "flawed ideas"—Lalo's words—about electricity.

"Don't stand near the sockets, sweet girl," she

told me when I visited, pulling me to the center of the room as if the electricity lurked in the sockets, waiting to hurl its arc forward. She always called me "sweet girl."

Lalo dropped his wool in the hallway and went looking for Sophie.

"How's your mother?" asked Mama, following him into the living room.

"At peace. There's no electricity," said Lalo.

Papa laughed.

Lalo saw Sophie. He smiled.

"So hello, Sophie."

"So, Lalo," said Sophie in a friendly, precise manner. "I want hot cereal."

"So how did that happen?" Lalo asked Mama, amazed.

Mama shook her head.

"Children speak at different times, in different ways," she said. "Larkin spoke early but never said her *d*'s."

"She called me 'Gaggy' instead of 'Daddy,' " said Papa.

"You hated it," said Mama, smiling at him. "You were insulted."

"Just think," said Lalo, "she has all these words inside her, all the things she's heard us say. She has *sentences* in her, sitting there, waiting to come out."

"Like your mother's electricity," I said, making Papa smile.

We all looked at Sophie, as if she were a book about to be opened. Or written, maybe.

"So we could teach her all sorts of things," said Lalo. He paused and looked at me. "Like poetry."

I frowned.

"Words. Just words," I said.

"Poetry?" Papa said softly. "Just words?" He looked at Mama.

"How do I love thee, let me count the ways . . ."

Mama looked up quickly. She smiled suddenly, a new look to her. Or an old look that I remembered.

"The fog comes in on little cat feet," said Byrd to Sophie.

"Cat feet," said Sophie. She pronounced the words carefully, like Ms. Minifred talking to Ozzie. We laughed. Sophie liked the sound of it, both the words and the laughter.

"Cat feet," she repeated.

We laughed again, and Papa put his arm around Mama. Sophie pulled at Papa's other hand. Mama and Papa got up, Mama lifting Sophie up too, Byrd's ruby around her neck gleaming on her blue pajamas. They danced together, the three of them. Sophie's arms went around them both as Lalo and Byrd and I watched, her small fat hands resting on their necks.

Lalo was quiet, watching.

They danced in the cold room to no music, though it seemed that music played.

"I like this," said Lalo.

Byrd smiled.

I liked it, too, Mama's face soft and smiling the way it used to be, Papa's arms around her. I wanted it to last forever, Mama and Papa dancing in slow circles, Sophie making them smile again.

Lalo moved closer to Byrd and me.

"Maybe Sophie will stay," he said after a moment, his voice soft.

I couldn't speak. Byrd reached over and took my hand.

Sophie cupped her hand and waved to me. I waved back, and there was a sudden sharp pain in my throat as I thought about Papa's warning not to love Sophie. *It's too late, Papa. Too late.* I looked quickly at Byrd and saw her face, her eyes dark and bright at the same time. It was too late for all of us.

The lights flickered then, and went on, and I held my breath, afraid that the dance would end. But only Sophie saw. She pointed to the lamp in the corner and, as if she, too, didn't want the moment to end, she whispered to us.

"There is light."

She remembered voices. And words like whispers in her ear. Words like the soft wind, touching her. Words.

chapter 11

The ice melted, the roads were cleared, and everything went back to the way it was. It was as if Mama and Papa hadn't put their arms around each other, as if Papa hadn't said words of poetry to her, as if Mama hadn't been happy for that little while.

Papa went back to his silences and his work and his nighttime tap-dancing on the tiles for Sophie. Mama went back to her studio, painting for the afternoon hours when Sophie napped. I didn't know what she was painting. There was no paint on her at the end of the day, no signs of what took her time, only a half smile when Papa asked her how it was going.

"Better," she said with a tilt of her head. "Hard, but better."

Byrd went back to her room behind the pocket doors, leaving them open wide enough for Sophie to walk in and out, and me, of course. Sophie dressed up in Byrd's velvet hat with the diamond clip, and the wide-brimmed straw with the long red ribbon, and lace and beads. And always the red ruby. They read books, Sophie talking and turning the pages and pointing. Byrd's voice was smooth, like the velvet of her hat.

"so much depends
upon

a red wheel
barrow

glazed with rain
water

beside the white
chickens."

"That's William Carlos Williams," Byrd said to Sophie.

"She doesn't understand," I said.

"She doesn't need to understand, dear," said Byrd. "She likes the way the words sound."

Sophie sat on the bed, Byrd's jet beads around her neck, the black velvet hat on her head. She looked at Byrd and pointed to the page.

"Read," she said. "Please."

Byrd smiled at me.

"She's not a baby anymore, you know. She's growing up."

"Not baby," said Sophie.

There was a small sound behind me and I turned. Mama was in the doorway watching.

"Not baby," Sophie said to Mama.

Mama looked at Sophie for a moment, as if studying her. Then she turned and was gone.

Sophie opened her hand and showed Byrd the ruby lying there.

Byrd looked at me. She sighed.

"Sophie should have that ruby," she said. "Don't you think, Larkin? Someday when I'm not here."

Someday. I swallowed.

81

"Larkin?"

"Yes," I said. "Yes."

"That's good," said Byrd, settling back with her book. She had a satisfied look, as if something had been settled. But it wasn't settled for me. I didn't want to think about someday. Someday Sophie might go away. Someday Byrd might not be here.

I watched Sophie lean back against Byrd and listen to Byrd read poetry.

Sophie looked up at me as Byrd read.

"Who has seen the wind?
Neither you nor I;
But when the trees bow down their heads
The wind is passing by."

"Wind," whispered Sophie. She held out her hands and did rock, paper, scissors.

Byrd smiled as she read and held out her hand and did the same, her wrinkled hand with the long fingers and the wide rose-gold wedding ring. Rock, paper, scissors.

82

When we went back to school Rebel had fixed the roof, Portia had new shining braces on her teeth, and Ms. Minifred wore red lipstick and large hanging gold earrings in the shape of half moons.

We went to the library for the last period of the day, and Lalo's mouth hung open when he saw Ms. Minifred.

"I thought she was *old,*" he whispered. "What happened?"

"Love happened," I said. "She is old. She just doesn't *look* old."

"No," said Lalo. "She looks wondrous."

She did look wondrous.

"Get ready for wondrous words," I said.

"Good afternoon. Sit up, Lalo. Remember the blood flow. Today poetry," said Ms. Minifred, smiling.

Words. Only words.

"I'm not going to lecture you about what poetry is, or how it's written," said Ms. Minifred. "Or even why it's written. You can look that up in books. Instead, I'm going to tell you a story about me."

Portia turned and smiled at Lalo and me; her braces and her glasses glittered. Ozzie didn't snort. He sat up, interested.

"And when my story is finished, class is over," said Ms. Minifred.

Rebel appeared from the hallway and leaned against the wall behind Ms. Minifred, his arms folded.

"When I was a girl, when I was twelve, my older brother William died," said Ms. Minifred. "I loved him. He was good to me. He read me stories and poetry. He wanted to be a writer, and he once said to me that words were comforting. Words had power, he told me. There was no way I could accept his death."

Ms. Minifred paused, and I felt a chill across my arms. No one moved. No one spoke. No one whispered. Rebel kept his eyes on Ms. Minifred.

"There was a funeral. There were flowers. Many people came, and many words were spoken. But their words didn't help. Their words had no power. I was angry," said Ms. Minifred. "I was

84

angry with my brother for leaving me." Ms. Minifred looked down at her hands. "I am still angry," she said softly. "And then I found a poem among my brother's books. He had marked this poem, so I knew it was important to him. When I read it I felt a strange and powerful comfort—not because it made me feel better, but because it said what I felt."

Ms. Minifred opened a book, an old book with worn pages.

"The poem is by Edna St. Vincent Millay. You may not understand it. That's all right. *I* understand it. And William understood it."

No one coughed or sneezed. Everyone was still. I thought of Byrd saying Sophie didn't have to understand the words.

"It is called 'Dirge Without Music.' "

Ms. Minifred began to read.

*"I am not resigned to the shutting away of loving hearts
    in the hard ground.*
*So it is and so it will be, for so it has been, time out of
    mind:*
*Into the darkness they go, the wise and the lovely.
    Crowned*

85

*With lilies and with laurel they go; but I am not re-
    signed.*

Lovers and thinkers, into the earth with you.
Be one with the dull, the indiscriminate dust.
A fragment of what you felt, of what you knew,
A formula, a phrase remains,—but the best is lost.

*The answers quick and keen, the honest look, the laughter,
    the love,—*
*They are gone. They are gone to feed the roses. Elegant
    and curled*
*Is the blossom. Fragrant is the blossom. I know. But I do
    not approve.*
*More precious was the light in your eyes than all the
    roses in the world.*

Down, down, down into the darkness of the grave
Gently they go, the beautiful, the tender, the kind;
Quietly they go, the intelligent, the witty, the brave.
I know. But I do not approve. And I am not resigned."

There was a terrible silence in the room. Ms.
Minifred put down the book very carefully. She
looked at us, but didn't say anything. We sat still,
staring at her.

After a moment Rebel stepped forward, standing in front of Ms. Minifred the way Lalo stood in front of me sometimes.

"Class is over," Rebel said quietly. "Go home."

chapter 12

I shut the front door softly, leaning against it, hardly breathing. Byrd's door was open, and when I walked past I saw her asleep, Sophie curled beside her. Lalo's voice echoed in my head. He had called to me as I got up from that library room and walked past Ms. Minifred and Rebel and out the door. He had called my name as I walked away from the school and then started to run toward home.

The house was quiet, and I knew Mama was in her studio. I went to Papa's book-lined study, shutting the door behind me. I found the book right away, *Collected Poems*, Edna St. Vincent Millay.

It had been read, I could tell. The pages had been turned and looked at and read, and I was angry suddenly, and frightened by it. The anger came up from my stomach and sat in my throat like a shout about to be let go. How could he have read this and not told me? All the months of *silence.* All the times we talked about stars and planets and Sophie. How could he?

I sat in the big chair by his desk and found the poem.

I am not resigned to the shutting away of loving hearts in the hard ground.

I put my hand over the page, hiding the words. All the way home I had thought that it was the library: that it was Ms. Minifred looking so wonderful and sad as she read, and most of all, Rebel coming forward to protect Ms. Minifred. But it wasn't. It wasn't just those things. It was the poem.

Into the darkness they go, the wise and the lovely.

I put the book facedown on the desk. Then, very slowly, I picked it up again and went out the

89

door and to Mama's studio. I didn't knock. I opened the door and walked in and saw Mama, and as if I dreamed it, she slowly turned from a painting, her mouth opening to ask me what was the matter, her eyes so blue in the north light of the room.

"Larkin! What's wrong?"

I gave her the book, opened to the poem, and the anger finally came out of me.

"I never saw the baby!" I said softly. "And you never named him!" I began to cry. My voice rose. "And you never talked to me about him!"

The tears came down my face and Mama took me in her arms, the book falling to the floor.

"Larkin, Larkin," she said over and over. "I didn't know."

"You should have known," I said, my voice muffled in her shoulder. "You're my mother."

Mama didn't say anything for a moment.

"I haven't been a good mother to you," she said softly.

I leaned back and looked at her.

"No, but you've been a good mother to Sophie," I said.

And then Mama began to cry, and she scared

me. It was as if she hadn't cried ever before and needed to make up all that time without tears. The tears came down her face and over my hair. We stood that way for a long time. And then Mama stopped and stepped back, wiping her eyes with the back of her hand. And I saw her easel behind her. There was a painting there, not finished, all bathed in white. There was light all around a small face with a tiny mouth, and the clear, dark eyes of a baby.

I stared at it for a long time.

"That's the way he was," she said.

I nodded. I stared at the painting for a long time. Then I looked up at Mama.

"Can we name him William?" I asked.

Mama didn't answer.

chapter 13

Sophie and I sat by the windows in Lalo's parents' big kitchen, Sophie patting the poinsettia plant on the table.

"That is red," I told her.

"That is red," she repeated.

Lalo's father was setting up the Christmas tree in the lobby, and from behind the closed kitchen door we could hear his father cursing loudly. Lalo grinned.

"Merry Christmas," he said.

Interested, Sophie looked up and pointed to the door as Marvella came rushing through, leaning on it as if to shut out his words.

"She didn't hear that, did she?" she asked, breathless. "He always curses when he puts up the Christmas tree."

"That's *our* family tradition," Lalo said to me.

"Man is not glad," said Sophie with a frown.

"Oh, dear," Marvella moaned. "Are you hungry, Sophie?"

Marvella hoped that food would interest Sophie. More loud words came from behind the door.

"Toast!" said Marvella loudly. "How about toast, sweet girls?"

Lalo got up and put a slice of bread in the toaster.

"Put slices in both sides remember, Lalo," said Marvella.

Lalo smirked at me.

"My mother thinks that if you don't fill up both sides of the toaster, electricity will leak out the empty side."

"Leakage," said Marvella, nodding.

The door opened and Lalo's father and Papa came in. Sophie looked up and smiled.

"Dammit," she said.

Papa and I walked home together, Sophie between us holding on to Papa's hand and mine. She wore her jacket and red boots, and we swung her up over puddles and curbs. The sun was behind a cloud, and the light slanted across the water and over the boats so that they looked like they'd been washed in silver. Herring gulls flew above us, and ringbills, too, with their fast, easy wing beats. Far off, the ferry came into sight. Sophie switched hands, walking backwards between us.

"You're silly, Sophie," said Papa, smiling at her.

"Silly Sophie," said Sophie.

Papa laughed.

"Silly Sophie," said Papa. "That's almost a poem."

"Yes," I said.

"Words," said Papa, softly. "Did you know that words have a life? They travel out into the air with the speed of sound, a small life of their own, before they disappear. Like the circles that a rock makes when it's tossed into the middle of the pond."

I smiled at the thought of it.

"You used to frown at words," said Papa.

"Until Ms. Minifred," I said.

"She walks in beauty, Ms. Minifred does," said Papa. "That's a poem."

"I know," I said. "I found it in your books."

Papa looked at me for a moment. We lifted Sophie high over a dog that lay sleeping on the sidewalk.

"I used to say that poem to your mother before she married me," said Papa. "I used to write her poems, and call her up to read poetry to her. Once, I stood under her window and shouted a Shakespeare sonnet to her until she threw a glass of water down on me."

I could feel my heart beating. Everything seemed still, even Sophie between us, the only sound the lonely cries of the gulls. I thought of Papa when he was young, trying to get Mama to love him with words.

"It would be good," I said, "if you still did that."

Papa looked quickly at me. Then he sighed, a sound that made Sophie look up at him.

"You grew up, Larkin," said Papa so softly

that I almost missed his words. "You grew up almost without me noticing."

Papa looked straight ahead, his face sad.

"And it wasn't behind my back, Lark." He sighed again. "It was right in front of me. And still I hardly saw it," he whispered.

I could feel tears in the corners of my eyes. "You were busy," I whispered, my throat tight.

Sophie looked at Papa, then at me.

"Busy," she whispered.

Papa stopped walking and dropped Sophie's hand. He gathered me up in his arms.

It had been a long time since he had held me like this, and I held on. I wound my legs around him and laid my head against his neck, and his smell that I remembered from when I was little finally made the tears come. Above, the birds cried, and Sophie reached over and took hold of my foot. But she didn't speak.

Papa kept me in his arms, holding me tighter, until the whistle of the ferry sounded when it passed the breakwater. Then, he bent down and picked up Sophie, holding the two of us. Sophie smiled and smiled at us, and the ferry came into the harbor.

"I love you, Lark," said Papa. "I love you."

"Love," said Sophie, touching Papa's mouth.

I thought about that word, *love*, with Papa's arms around me. That word with a life of its own, traveling out over the town, over the water, out into the world, flying above all of us like the birds.

Love.

spring

There were clouds in all her dreams. She liked their names: cirrus, cumulus, and another one just out of reach of her memory. She didn't remember ever learning the names of clouds.

Sometimes she thought she was born knowing them.

chapter 14

"There are three things to remember about spring on the island," old man Brick said. "One, it comes after winter. Two, it comes after winter. Three, it comes after winter and you think it's still winter."

Island winters were always long, flurries of snow when what we had longed for were drifts of it, rain when we wanted sun. Spring came after without change, except for more rain that made us cold.

"Cold to the bone," said Byrd.

She got out the black lace long underwear

she'd decorated with jewels and wore it from October to June.

Mama loved spring. Papa liked it because the island was still empty of tourists. But Mama saw color.

"That's wonderful, look! Pink, and that wonderful warm gray. Violet and mauve!" she said.

Mama made Lalo smile.

"Your mother is not trustworthy," he said. "So, just remember your Christmas tree."

Papa laughed. Sophie had helped trim the tree, carefully setting large untidy wads of cotton on one side. Mama wouldn't allow anyone to change it.

"It's Sophie's Christmas too," she said firmly.

Lalo thought it was the ugliest tree he had ever seen, and he said so.

"It is very tasteless," he said admiringly.

"There's some redundancy there," I said, echoing Rebel.

The tree had leaned to one side all through Christmas, finally falling in a heap on New Year's Day, glass balls breaking and the lights going out with a final flash.

A Christmas letter and package had come for

Sophie, delivered two weeks late because of wind-storms that kept the ferry in port and the planes on the ground. Papa read us the letter.

> *Dearest Sophie,*
> *I think of you and miss you. Things are better.*
> *Love,*
> *Mama*

Things are better. None of Sophie's mother's letters had ever said that. Each month she wrote, sometimes twice a month, always saying the same things: I love you, I miss you. But no letter had ever said things are better.

Byrd got up and walked to the window, pulling a curtain aside to look out.

"It was a good Christmas with Sophie here," she said, her voice sounding far away and unsteady.

Mama unwrapped the package, a small rubber doll in a red dress. She handed it to Sophie. Sophie turned it over in her hand. She pulled a leg off.

"Baby leg," she said.

She smiled and pulled the other one off.

103

Mama leaned over and took Sophie in her arms.

Papa looked at me quickly, then went off to work. And winter slipped into spring with those words—*things are better*—always with us, following us like clouds over our heads.

When it came to Mama that it was really, truly spring, she made us bundle up for the beach. Every spring she took her easel and paints to the beach before tourists came. She packed picnic lunches, and we pretended it was warm.

"It's April, love," Mama told Papa cheerfully. "Let's go."

"This is your mother's robust time of year," said Papa grumpily, pulling on his hat with the ear flaps.

"Well, I'm not going," said Byrd. "I'm going to sit by the fire."

"Sophie's going," said Mama slyly.

"That's unfair," said Byrd.

Byrd got up and put on her boots with the fleece lining and her wool hat, and we all went.

Papa carried Sophie on his shoulders, Mama carried her paint box. We walked through town.

"Hello, you foolish people!" called Griffey from his sewer truck. "Hello there, Sophie!"

"Hello, Sophie!" yelled Sophie.

Marvella waved from the inn window, watching our procession, and Lalo came out on the porch.

"Is it spring?" he called excitedly. "Wait for me!"

He disappeared and came out wearing the new red wool scarf that Marvella had knitted for him. It wound around his neck several times, another wool barrier from germs, and trailed behind him on the ground.

Lalo saw Papa smiling at it.

"My mother was overcome by knitting during the winter," said Lalo, winding the scarf around his neck one more time. "Totally overcome," he added, peering sideways at me. "I know that's redundant. My mother is redundant."

"You look splendid, dear," said Byrd. "Rather like the cavalry."

She took Lalo's arm and we walked on.

"Besides," she said softly, "that scarf may save us all from freezing."

Old man Brick passed us, his ancient truck lurching. Then we heard a motorcycle. Lalo looked at me as Rebel came down the main street. On the back of his motorcycle was Ms. Minifred, her hair blowing out under her red and white striped helmet. They waved. We waved.

"Hello, Eunice!" Mama called.

Lalo and I stopped walking suddenly.

"Eunice?" I said. "Ms. Minifred's name is Eunice?"

Lalo grinned.

"She rides in beauty, Eunice Minifred does," said Papa, putting his arm around Mama, as Ms. Minifred and Rebel roared down the street.

"Yep," said Lalo, laughing.

"Yep," I said.

"Yep," said Sophie.

The water was blue and green, the sky clear except for high clouds that made me think of Sophie's cotton wads on the Christmas tree. We found a place by a dune, out of the wind that blew

106

the sand along the beach. Byrd sat back, leaning against a driftwood log, Lalo close next to her, the scarf draped around them like a red snake.

"It's too windy for painting," said Mama, taking out her sketchbook.

Papa walked off a bit, looking out over the water. Sanderlings raced the waves, always just ahead of them, their heads bobbing as they fed. On the rocks were purple sandpipers, left over from winter. Black-bellied plovers flew to the beach, settled, then flew off again.

Papa turned and smiled and held out his hand to Sophie. She ran to him, her hat flying off in the wind. Papa picked it up and took her hand. The two of them walked slowly down the beach, the clouds behind them as large as mountains.

"It looks like they're walking into a painting," I said.

Byrd and Mama turned at the same time, watching Papa bend down and point to the sky. Sophie put her hand on his shoulder and looked up. Far away, cormorants flew close to the water in a line. Behind them the ferry moved slowly toward us. Papa sat down with Sophie on his lap. He bent his head and talked to her for a long time. They both looked up at the sky. The wind died then, and the sun came out from behind the big cloud, and there was that sudden silence that comes when the waves stop crashing.

"Oh, my," whispered Byrd.

I watched Mama look at Papa and Sophie. There was a look about her that was half happy, half sad.

"Spring," Mama whispered back.

Ms. Minifred said once that life is made up of circles.

"Life is not a straight line," she said. "And sometimes we circle back to a past time. But we are not the same. We are changed forever."

I didn't understand what she meant then. I remember steam whistling in the radiator under the window in the school library, and the way Ms. Minifred's hair brushed the side of her face when she leaned forward. But I liked the sound of her words, and I remember saving them for later.

Sophie didn't want to leave the beach, but Papa picked her up, wailing, and we slowly walked back through town. When she stopped crying

108

Papa put her down. Sophie stood there frowning at him, her forehead wrinkled with the effort. After a moment she reached up and took his hand.

"Forgiveness," said Papa to Mama.

The two of them walked ahead of us as the light began to fade from the sky, Sophie's red boots making a slapping sound on the sidewalk. And then, suddenly, Sophie began to shuffle. "Me and My Shadow." We stopped, Mama laughing. People passing by smiled, too, and Papa began to dance with her. Papa smiled at Mama over Sophie's head, and the sky darkened into dusk. Finally, Papa swooped Sophie up in his arms and we began to walk home. We started up the hill to our house. Dry grass crunched under our feet.

And when Lalo and I ran ahead of them through the meadow of dry chickory and meadowsweet, when we climbed up and over the rise to my house, she was sitting in the darkness of the porch. Sophie's mother.

Life is made up of circles.

chapter 15

Lalo and I stopped. We both knew. Lalo, as if remembering a cue from the past, moved in front of me. Byrd came up quietly beside us, and I turned to tell her. But she knew too. I could tell by the steady look she gave the woman on the porch and the stillness that came over her face. Byrd lifted her shoulders and pulled her jacket around her, smoothing it over the buttons as if she was preparing for something. Behind us, below the crest of the hill, Mama laughed, and we could hear Papa's voice.

I clenched my teeth. I wanted to turn and call

to Papa and Mama to take Sophie away, to turn and run as fast as they could. Lalo knew it, because he took my hand and held it to keep me there.

"Larkin," he whispered.

There was a silence. The woman on the porch didn't move.

"Larkin," he said again. He said it in a way I'd never heard before. It was the saddest sound, as if he was trying to say he knew how bad this was and to protect me at the same time, trying to wrap my name around me like his long wool scarf.

And then we heard the sound of Sophie's high voice. The woman on the porch rose suddenly from the chair and walked to the edge of the porch into the late light of the day. She held on to the porch post, and we all turned as Mama and Papa and Sophie came up the path.

Mama walked ahead of Papa and Sophie, Sophie on Papa's shoulders. Mama walked up to us with a questioning look as we stood there.

"What—?" she began, and then she saw Sophie's mother.

It was like a movie run slowly: Byrd putting

out her hand, Mama's face showing the slow recognition, her face slipping, like Byrd's, into a mask that didn't look like Mama anymore; Mama moving away from Byrd, taking a step toward Papa, away from the woman who didn't see the rest of us anymore. All in that moment.

"Sophie," the woman whispered.

Papa stumbled a little, and then he stood still, looking at Sophie's mother. After a moment he walked up to Mama. He stared at her, and then put his arm around Mama. Sophie leaned over, smiling at this, her hands patting Mama's head.

"My baby," the woman said.

And Sophie straightened. She looked over and studied the woman for a moment.

"Not baby," said Sophie.

And on the porch her mother's face slowly crumpled. She burst into tears, sitting on the porch steps, her hands over her face.

Byrd took a breath and moved, but Mama's voice stopped her.

"Sophie?" Mama reached up and took Sophie down from Papa's shoulders. She carried Sophie over to the porch and sat down beside the woman. I looked at Papa and watched the way he looked at

Mama. And then Mama said the words that were the hardest to say.

"This is your mama."

I can never forget the small things, the tiny gestures, the look of Mama's eyes, Papa's face, the way Byrd sat so still and careful as if a breeze might topple her. Sometimes these things play over and over in my head like the notes and rhythms of a song.

Our coats hung in the hallway closet. Our boots were lined up in pairs, except for Sophie's. Papa poked at the fire, moved a log, then poked again. He hung the fire poker on a hook, and it fell on the hearth in a clatter that made us all jump. Byrd sat in a straight chair, her legs crossed at the ankles, Mama on the sofa. Sophie's mother stood staring at Sophie, who wore her boots and a sweater Marvella had knitted for her, the too-long sleeves rolled at her wrists. Sophie sat on the floor and slowly began to build a tower with her blocks. Red on blue on green.

"Julia?" Mama said.

Julia. It was hard to think of Sophie's mother

1 1 3

with a name. We had always called her Sophie's mother.

Mama held a cup of tea out to her.

"Now," said Mama.

Julia sighed, then looked at Lalo and me standing by the front door.

"Maybe we should talk alone," she said.

Her voice was low and soft. Sophie looked up at her suddenly, her hands stopped above the blocks. *That look.* Does she remember her mother? Does she miss her? I had asked Mama that a long time ago. *That look.* Lalo moved a little beside me, the smallest movement, like a sigh.

"No," said Byrd very quietly, so quietly that we all looked at her. All of us except for Sophie, who stared at her mother.

"Everyone here has been Sophie's family since"—Byrd paused—"since you left her," said Byrd.

Julia winced. She sat down by the fireplace.

"Everyone here has rocked her and read to her and wiped her tears and sung to her. Lalo taught her how to blow a kiss, and sometimes she slept with Larkin. She painted with Lily and she danced with John." Byrd paused. "Everyone here has been her family."

There was silence.

Julia looked at Byrd, and then at Lalo and me, studying us for a moment. She turned back to Byrd.

"That is why I chose you," she said softly.

And then, for the first time, she smiled. Lalo turned his head to look at me. I couldn't look at him, but I knew what his look meant. Julia's smile was Sophie's smile.

Papa sat down next to Mama. He reached over and took her hand. They looked at Julia.

Julia began to speak.

"I watched you last summer, all of you," she said.

Sophie got up from the floor and moved closer to the fire.

"Hot," Julia said almost without thinking.

Sophie looked up.

"Fire is hot," she said.

Julia stared at her.

"Sophie talks," she whispered.

"Sophie talks," whispered Sophie back to her.

Julia swallowed. Tears sat in the corners of her eyes.

"Sophie's father was sick," she whispered. "We knew he would need an operation, and we knew that he would need care all the time. All *my* time. If he didn't die. There was no one else. That was when I saw you."

She stopped then, and looked at Byrd.

"And my parents were not good parents," she said in a flat voice. "I never would have let them have Sophie. Never. I didn't want Sophie to be with strangers. And you didn't feel like strangers."

"You wrote—" began Mama, but her voice broke. "You wrote that things are better."

"Sophie's father will get well," said Julia.

Papa moved on the sofa.

"You took a great risk," he said.

It was the first time he had spoken.

Julia looked at him, then at the rest of us.

"But that is what a mother does," she said.

No one spoke.

I wanted to hate her. I wanted her to go away and leave Sophie with us. I didn't ever want to see her again. Ever. But I couldn't hate her, because in the silence of the room Sophie walked over to her

116

mother. She didn't speak. They stared at each other for a moment. Then Sophie put her hand out and Sophie's mother took it, and Sophie began to move her hand up and down. Something familiar from long ago.

Tears came down Papa's cheeks.

Circles.

The ferry stood at the dock. It looked old and worn in the light of morning, all of its rust and sea-streaked paint showing. The wind blew in gusts, some so harsh that Byrd held on to Lalo's arm. Three cars and an empty flatbed truck went on the ferry, making a lonely clatter on the metal gangplank. A handful of people walked on, turning to wave to the handful on the wharf. Papa held Sophie tightly, and walked away from us, farther down the wharf. Sophie pointed up to the sky. Papa spoke to her, and she smiled.

I saw Griffey, Rollie, and Arthur back by the gas pump looking strange without their instruments. Old man Brick sat in his truck, looking through the windshield. He didn't get out. Lalo's mother and father walked down the sidewalk, and

Dr. Fortunato's car drove in and stopped where the wooden wharf began. He opened the door and stood next to it, watching us. Rebel sat on his motorcycle, and Ms. Minifred got off the back. A gust of wind came up, and her hair blew across her face. Without looking at her Rebel handed her his scarf.

Julia turned to Mama.

"Thank you is all there's left to say," she said.

Mama took her hand, then they both looked at Papa.

"John."

Mama said his name softly, but even in the wind he heard.

He stood still for a moment. Then he kissed Sophie. He walked back to us. He handed Sophie to her mother. Byrd reached over and put the necklace with the ruby around Sophie's neck.

Julia turned and walked onto the ferry. Sophie stared at us over her back. Her eyes were solemn. I looked quickly at Papa, and he stared at Sophie as if he were trying to memorize her. Sophie didn't smile. But just before she disappeared inside she reached over Julia's back and held out her hand to Papa. A small fist. Beside me Papa's hand did paper, scissors, back to her. It was then that Sophie smiled.

chapter 16

We walked up the hill in silence, through the field, past the pond where the wind sent ripples across the water. Even Lalo didn't talk. The wind caught Byrd's hat once, and Papa grabbed it. He handed it back without words.

The house was cool. The smell of dead ashes hung in the air. Papa went to the fireplace and stood there, looking down as if waiting for the fire to blaze again. Mama took off her hat and leaned against the front door, staring into the room. Byrd bent down and picked up a book. Sophie's book. Byrd straightened.

"We are going to talk now," she said softly.

Papa turned. "Not now," he said. His face had the look of his business face, but his voice was thin, like a thread of smoke.

Mama took off her coat and walked to her studio door.

"You cannot walk away and leave this behind as if it never happened," said Byrd. She paused. "Like the baby."

Mama stopped. Papa stared at Byrd. I stared too. And then the ferry whistle blew, a terrible soft sound behind the closed door. Papa flinched, and in that moment his business look was gone.

It was quiet when the sound ended, and I could hear Lalo breathing beside me.

"That's why we're going to talk," said Byrd softly.

Mama's face changed then. She looked transparent, as if all her feelings were there right under her skin. I heard the front door opening and closing, and when I turned Lalo had left.

"Come. Sit down," said Byrd. Her voice had changed, and it sounded almost friendly, like a pleasant invitation.

No one moved.

"I'll sit, then," said Byrd. "I'm old," she added.

Byrd moved to the straight chair by the fireplace. She looked at me.

"If we talk about Sophie, we can talk about Larkin's brother who died. The baby she never saw. The baby with no name."

I walked across the room and sat on the couch.

"Words," Byrd said.

She smiled slightly and I gathered courage from that.

"Even *Sophie* had words," I said.

Papa studied me for a moment, then he looked at Mama across the room. He let out a breath, as if he'd been holding it for a long time. He went over and took Mama's hand.

"Words, Lily," he whispered to her. "Not painting. Not dancing. *Words.*" Mama was so quiet, like a statue that might break apart if it were touched.

Papa put his arm around her. He looked at me. Then he began to speak.

"His eyes were dark blue, Larkin," he said softly. "So dark, but bright at the same time. Like stars," he whispered.

I stared at Papa. Byrd moved a little beside me.

122

Mama looked up at Papa. "His hands," she said softly. "His hands had long fingers, like Larkin's. And he had a serious, thoughtful look."

I looked out the window and I could see the distant smoke from the ferry. Then Mama came to sit by me. And in the cool still room, as the ferry took Sophie away, we named the baby William.

It had been warm in the cemetery, the late afternoon sun low in the sky. Light slanted over us and the gravestones, making us all look the same, stones and people. The only sound was the sound of waves on the outer beach, waves one after the other, like heartbeats.

Everyone had come and gone; Griffey and Rollie and the boys who had played a song, Dr. Fortunato, Ms. Minifred and Rebel, who had put a rose on the small gravestone that had WILLIAM engraved on it. And Lalo, who had cried. Byrd had cried, too, when Papa said his words about William.

"I wish I could have danced with him," he said.

Mama had put her arms around Byrd, and they had stood there in that light as everyone went down the hill.

Afterward, we walked home through town, past the stores and houses.

"Will we see her again?" I asked Byrd. "Sophie?"

No one looked surprised. Papa smiled at me. It was easier to talk about Sophie now.

"Yes," said Byrd. "You'll see her again. Sometime."

Mama looked sideways at Byrd and smiled. She stopped.

"Remember walking home with Sophie?" she said. "After we'd been to the beach? Right about there"—she pointed—"and about this time of day, Sophie began to dance."

I walked ahead of them and turned, looking at Byrd, her hair like silver in the light, at Mama and Papa holding hands, at Lalo with his look that seemed to say *I know what you're going to do.* And he did, of course.

I began to do the soft shoe. Papa and Mama stared at me, Papa's eyes widening. Byrd smiled.

Me and my shadow
Strolling down the avenue.
Me and my shadow
Not a soul to tell our troubles to.

"I learned," I said. I grinned at the sight of them all, standing there so still and so surprised. And then, for some reason, as I danced I began to cry.

summer—
ten years later

The memories came all the time now, crowding in, filling her head. They came in mist and clouds, almost revealing what was hidden behind them. Clouds with a face nearly hidden. Clouds.

And that face.

chapter 17

We leaned on the boat railing as land came into sight. Birds followed the boat, wheeling above and over it. One herring gull came so close, we could almost touch it. The day was crisp for summer. I turned to look at Sophie as she studied the island. She looked at the cliffs at the far end, then at the town that we could see clearly now, the harbor, the church, the hill where the cemetery was.

Sophie was tall, almost up to my shoulder. Her hair had lost the fair baby color. Now it was the same color as mine. Around her neck was the chain with the red ruby.

Sophie turned to her mother.

"Did you spend a lot of time here?" she asked.

"Only that summer," said Julia. "That summer," she repeated softly, like an echo. Julia looked at me and we smiled.

The boat passed the breakwater and Sophie's hands went up to cover her ears just before the whistle blew.

"You remembered the whistle," I said.

"Did I?" said Sophie. "Sometimes—" Sophie stopped for a moment, then went on. "Sometimes I remember things and I don't know what they mean." Sophie turned and looked at me with the familiar look that made *me* remember her. "I remember a face," she said.

The boat came into the harbor, and Sophie took the newspaper clipping out of her pocket. It was folded over and worn from reading and rereading. It told of the life, the death, and where the burial would be.

Byrd.

"Will I know them?" asked Sophie. "Will they know me?"

Julia smiled.

"You've seen pictures," she said. "And all

those letters." She paused. "Probably yes. Somehow you'll know them."

"They'll know you," I said.

The boat came slowly up to the dock. The lines were tossed and tied. Then we walked down the stairs and onto the landing.

"Do they know I'll be here?" asked Sophie.

I shook my head.

"I didn't know if you'd come," I said.

We walked down the sidewalk, past the stores and houses, and past Lalo's parents' inn. Sophie stopped and looked down at the sidewalk. My heart beat faster.

"You danced here," I said.

Sophie didn't say anything. Then, she reached over and took my hand. We walked along to the grassy place where the cemetery began. Julia stopped and touched Sophie's arm.

"You go ahead," she said.

Sophie looked at her.

"It's all right," said Julia. She smiled. "It will be fine," she said softly.

There were people standing at the top of the hill, their backs to us. We walked up the hill still holding hands. Sophie looked back once, at her mother waiting at the bottom of the hill, looking so small. Then, when we had almost reached the graveside, and we could hear the murmur of low voices, Sophie looked up at the high, thin clouds.

"Mares' tails," she said suddenly. "Mares' tails."

Lalo turned at Sophie's voice. His eyes widened. He grinned at us.

Sophie grinned too. And then, suddenly, Sophie stopped and stared.

Mares' tails. Mares' tails, and walking in the sand by the water, the wind taking her hat, and the man's whisper in her ear. Mares' tails and the face.

Papa stood next to a small gravestone with the name WILLIAM engraved on it. He didn't see Sophie. But, just before the minister began to speak Sophie dropped my hand and walked up to Papa. He turned and stared down at her. She smiled at him. She held out her hand.

Rock.

Paper.

Scissors.

ANOTHER YEARLING FAVORITE BY PATRICIA MACLACHLAN

JOURNEY

Journey is eleven the summer his mother leaves him and his sister, Cat, with their grandparents. He is sad and angry, and spends the summer looking for the clues that will explain why she left.

Journey searches photographs for answers. He hunts for family resemblances in Grandma's albums. Looking for happier times, he tries to put together the torn pieces of the pictures his mother shredded before her departure. And he also searches the photographs his grandfather takes as the older man attempts to provide Journey with a past. In the process, the boy learns to look and finds that, for him, the camera is a means of finding things his naked eye has missed—things like the inevitability of his mother's departure and the love that still binds his family.

An American Library
Association Notable Book
for Children

An American Library
Association Best Book for
Young Adults

♦ "Vintage MacLachlan: uniquely memorable people; a funny, pungent, compact, and wonderfully wise story."—*Kirkus Reviews*, Pointer

Mama named me Journey. Journey, as if somehow she wished her restlessness on me. But it was Mama who would be gone the year that I was eleven—before spring crashed onto our hillside with explosions of mountain laurel, before summer came with the soft slap of the screen door, breathless nights, and mildew on the books. I should have known, but I didn't. My older sister Cat knew. Grandma knew, but Grandma kept it to herself. Grandfather knew and said so.

Mama stood in the barn, her suitcase at her feet.

"I'll send money," she said. "For Cat and Journey."

"That's not good enough, Liddie," said Grandfather.

"I'll be back, Journey," my mother said softly.

But I looked up and saw the way the light trembled in her hair, making her look like an angel, someone not earthbound. Even in that moment she was gone.

"No, son," Grandfather said to me, his voice loud in the barn. "She won't be back."

And that was when I hit him.

Chapter One

MY GRANDFATHER is belly down in the meadow with his camera, taking a close-up of a cow pie. He has, in the weeks since Mama left, taken many photographs—one of our least trustworthy cow, Mary Louise, standing up to her hocks in meadow muck; one of my grandmother in the pantry, reading a book while bees, drawn to her currant wine, surround her head in a small halo; and many of himself, taken with the self-timer device he's not yet figured out. The pictures of himself fascinate him. They line the back of the barn wall in a series of my grandfather in flight, dressed in overalls, caught in the moment of entering the picture, or leaving it; some with grand dimwitted smiles, his hair flying; one of a long, work-worn hand stretched out gracefully, the only part of him able to make it into the frame before the camera clicks.

Cat gave him the camera in one of her fits of cleanliness.

"I've given up the camera," she yelled, her head underneath the bed, unearthing her life. "I've given up the flute and most everything else. Including meat," she said pointedly. "I have spent the entire afternoon looking into the eyes of a cow, and have become a vegetarian."

"Which cow?" asked my grandmother, not kidding.

Cat gave her a quick look. Grandfather picked up Cat's camera and peered through the lens.

"You tired of this, Cat?"

Cat sighed.

"My pictures are so . . ." She waved her hand to the pile of pictures. "So . . ."

"Boring," Grandfather finished for her.

I felt my face flush with anger, but Cat laughed.

"Take it, Grandpa," she said cheerfully.

Grandfather turned to me.

"Journey?"

"No."

What did he think I'd take pictures of? This farm? I could close my eyes and see it—the spruce trees at the edge of the meadow, the stream cutting through, the stone walls that framed it all. I knew every inch of every acre. What would pictures tell me? And the people. What would pictures tell me of my grandmother, so secretive; my grandfather, tall and blunt?

On Cat's dresser was a picture of our father who had gone away somewhere a long time ago. He was young in the picture, laughing, his eyes looking past the camera, past the place, past me. When I was little, I carried that picture around, trying to remember him, trying to place the picture so that the eyes would look into mine. But they never did. His face was like carved stone, not flesh and blood. And the picture never told me the things I wanted to know.

Did he think about Cat and me? Where was he? Would I know him if I saw him?

I turned and the camera clicked: Grandfather's first picture of me. I stared at him angrily, and slowly he lowered the camera and looked at me with a surprised and dismayed expression, as if he'd seen something through the lens that he hadn't expected.

Grandma's voice broke the silence.

"I'll take the flute, Cat. And this."

Grandma had put on the sweatshirt that Mama had given Cat, LIDDIE written across the front in big letters.

"No!" My voice sounded harsher than I meant. "That's Mama's shirt!"

Grandfather put his hand on my shoulder.

"Your mama left it, Journey."

I shook off his hand and stepped away from him.

Grandma stood in the light of the window, her hair all tumbled like Mama's in the barn. I looked at Cat to see if she noticed, but Cat was smiling at Grandma.

"You look wonderful, Gran."

Cat pulled me after her and went to hug

Grandma. And Grandfather took a picture that would startle me every time I saw it: not Grandma, her hair tied back with a piece of string, smiling slightly as if she knew the secrets of the world; not Cat, her head thrown back, laughing; but my face, staring into the camera with such fury that even in the midst of the light and the laughter the focus of the picture is me.

Chapter Two

The first letter that wasn't a letter came in the noon mail. It lay in the middle of the kitchen table like a dropped apple, addressed to Cat and me, Mama's name in the left-hand corner.

I'd watched Cat walk up the front path from the mailbox, slowly, as if caught by the camera in slow motion or in a series of what Grandfather called stills: Cat smiling. Cat looking eager. Cat, her face suddenly unfolding out of a smile. She brushed past me at the front door and opened her hand, the letter falling to the table.

"No return address," she said flatly.

My grandmother stirred soup on the stove and looked sideways at me. After a moment she looked away again.

Grandfather, cleaning his camera lens with lens paper, lifted his shoulders in a sigh, the way he always did when he was about to say something I didn't want to hear.

"I expect—" he began.

Grandma's voice made me jump.

"Marcus!" Then softer. "Let it be."

Cat began to cut carrots at the kitchen counter. My grandfather flinched with each violent stroke.

"I think (thwack) that what Grandpa (thwack) means is that there will be (thwack) money in that envelope. Not words."

Cat stopped and stared down at the counter, the sudden silence like noise filling the room.

"Not the words you want," Cat said softly.

I felt tears behind my eyes. There was something soft and sad in Cat's voice that made me think of Mama.

Grandma stopped stirring the soup, and Grandfather cleared his throat.

"You will be disappointed," he said.

"I'm not disappointed," I said loudly. "I'm not!"

I reached over and tore off one end of the envelope, blowing inside the way Grandfather always did.

Inside were two small packets of money, the bills fastened with paper clips and a torn piece of paper on each. One said CAT. The other said JOURNEY. The paper clip over my name was bent, as if Mama might have tried to make it right and hadn't. I stared at that paper clip for a long time.

"There are words," I said. My voice rose. "There are words! Our names are there. Our names are words!"

There was silence. The sound of my voice hung in the air between us. Cat turned to face me.

"Journey, you keep the money. Do whatever you want with it."

She began to cut the carrots again, this time calm and steady.

"I'll put it in the bank," I said. Grandma

smiled at me from the stove. Grandfather peered at her through his camera and snapped a picture. I stood, suddenly angry, wanting him to stop taking pictures.

"I'll start a travel account!" I shouted.

Surprised, Grandfather put down his camera.

"So that when Mama tells us where she is, Cat and I can go visit! We'll take a bus . . . or a train. Something fast."

I looked down at the letter in my hand.

"She forgot the return address," I said.

Cat turned at the counter to stare at me.

"She forgot, that's all," I said softly.

Grandma wiped her hands on her apron and came over and put her arms around me. I smelled onion and something like flowers, lilacs maybe, and I burst into tears.

"Ah, Journey," Grandma murmured.

I heard the click of Grandfather's camera.

"Why does he do that?" I asked, my voice muffled in Grandma's shoulder. I leaned back to look at Grandfather. "Why do you do that? Why?"

"Because he needs to," said Grandma softly.

"I don't understand."

"I know," she whispered.

*   *   *

My bedroom was sun-dappled and quiet, the smell of lilacs strong through the open window, mingling with the lily-of-the-valley from under the bush outside.

"Journey?"

The door opened and Grandma stood there with a bowl of soup in one hand, an album in the other. She set the bowl on the table by my bed. Then she opened the album. It was full of pictures, pictures of people I didn't know—men in black suits and white starched shirts and broad-brimmed hats, women in flowered dresses, and children with bows as big as balloons in their hair. Grandma pointed.

"Me," she said, "when I was Cat's age."

In the picture Grandma sat in the garden swing, looking straight at the camera with a great smile on her face. Tables were set up in the garden with food and pitchers and bowls of flowers.

"This was taken on a long-ago Fourth of July." Grandma closed her eyes. "Nineteen thirty, I think. The day I met your grandfather."

"You look happy," I said.

Grandma nodded and looked at the picture.

"The camera knows," she said.

"The camera knows what?"

She turned more pages.

"And here is your mother, same age, same day, but many years later. Grandpa took that picture. He didn't have so fine a camera as now, of course."

In the picture the girl who was my mama sat behind a table, her face in her hands, looking far off in the distance. All around her were people laughing, talking. Lancie, Mama's sister, made a face at the camera. Uncle Minor, his hair all sunbleached, was caught by the camera taking a handful of cookies. In the background a dog leaped into the air to grab a ball, his ears floating out as if uplifted and held there by the wind. But my mother looked silent and unhearing.

"It's a nice picture," I said. "Except for Mama. It must have been the camera," I said after a moment.

Grandma sighed and took my hand.

"No, it wasn't the camera, Journey. It was your mama. Your mama always wished to be somewhere else."

"Well, now she is," I said.

After a while Grandma got up and left the room. I sat there for a long time, staring at Mama's picture, as if I could will her to turn and talk to the person next to her. If I looked at the picture long enough, my mama would move, stretch, smile at my grandfather behind the camera. But she didn't. I turned away, but her face stayed with me. The expression on Mama's face was one I knew. One I remembered.

Somewhere else. I am very little, five or six, and in overalls and new yellow rubber boots. I follow Mama across the meadow. It has rained and everything is washed and shiny, the sky clear. As I walk my feet make squishing sounds, and when I try to catch up with Mama I fall into the brook. I am not afraid, but when I look up Mama has walked away. Arms pick me up, someone else's arms. Someone else takes off my boots and pours out the water. My grandfather. I am angry. It is not my grandfather I want. It is Mama. But Mama is far ahead, and she doesn't look back. She is somewhere else.

I walked to the window. Birds still sang, flowers still bloomed, cows still slept in the meadow, and I ate soup—now cold—as if my mama hadn't ever gone.